Dragonflies

Molly McLaughlin

Walker and Company ✺ New York

For Zack

Special thanks are due to John Alcock, Ola M. Fincke, Michael May and Curtis E. Williams for generously sharing their knowledge and enthusiasm about dragonflies; and to the photographers whose pictures provide such unforgettable views of these fascinating insects.

I would also like to thank members of the library staff at the Academy of Natural Sciences in Philadelphia for their help with research for this book.

Text copyright © 1989 by Molly McLaughlin

First published in the United States of America in 1989 by the Walker Publishing Company, Inc.

Published simultaneously in Canada by Thomas Allen & Son Canada, Limited, Markham, Ontario

Library of Congress Cataloging-in-Publication Data

McLaughlin, Molly.
   Dragonflies / Molly McLaughlin.
      p.   cm.
   Summary: Text and photographs reveal the life cycle of dragonflies.
   ISBN 0-8027-6846-6. ISBN 0-8027-6847-4 (lib. bdg.)
   1. Dragonflies—Juvenile literature. [1. Dragonflies.]
I. Title.
QL520.M35   1989   595.7′33—dc19   88-20632

Printed in Hong Kong

10 9 8 7 6 5 4 3 2 1

Book design by Laurie McBarnette

Dragonflies

Top left to bottom: *The final two hours in a dragonfly's change from drab wingless creature to graceful flier. The new adult dragonfly struggles free from its outgrown skin and waits for its wings and body to dry.*

Very early on a summer morning, a ferocious-looking six-legged creature crawls out of a pond and up a plant stem. For half an hour it clings there, not moving.

Then a slight bulge appears behind the creature's head. The bulge grows bigger and bigger, until at last the hard skin of the creature's back splits open.

Slowly a new creature struggles out. Soft and pale, with damp, crumpled-up wings and bulging eyes, it rests quietly next to its old, empty skin.

Soon the wings open, spread out, and begin to dry. The body hardens. The insect stays on the stem as the sun climbs higher and the air gets warm. Finally, on new wings that glisten in the sunlight, it darts up and flies away.

Striking colors and distinctive wing and body shapes help dragonflies and damselflies recognize mates and rivals. **This page:** Three dragonflies. **Top:** Candle-flame skimmer. **Center:** Five-striped leaftail. **Bottom:** Twelve-spot skimmer. **Opposite** (Page 3): Three damselflies. **Top:** Sparkling jewelwing. **Center:** Spine-tipped dancer. **Bottom:** Desert firetail.

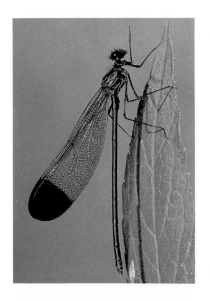

This is the first flight of a newly grown-up dragonfly. Dragonflies are spectacular and fascinating insects that have lived on earth for a very long time.

Three hundred million years ago, before the great dinosaurs roamed the earth, before there were birds or flowering plants, ancestors of the dragonflies were gliding through the air. They sailed on rigid wings almost three feet across. These ancient creatures were the biggest insects the world has ever seen.

By the time of the dinosaurs, one hundred eighty million years ago, there were dragonflies very much like those we see today. Through all these ages, conditions on earth have changed a great deal, but dragonflies have not changed very much at all.

Modern dragonflies and their close relatives, the damselflies, are large insects, beautifully decorated with jewel-like colors and flashy markings. They live by hunting and eating other insects. Though not as huge as the original dragonflies of long ago, they are still among the world's biggest flying insects, with bodies up to four inches long and wings up to five inches across.

There are over 4,000 different kinds, or *species,* of dragonflies and damselflies. Dragonflies have broad bodies and their enormous eyes cover the fronts of their faces. Damselflies' bodies are more slender and delicate, and their eyes are at the sides of their heads. When dragonflies rest, they hold their long, narrow wings out to the side like tiny gliders. Most damselflies fold their wings up over their backs. The word "dragonfly" is often used to mean both dragonflies and damselflies.

Eastern amberwing in flight. Dragonflies and damselflies alternate wings when they fly, moving the front pair up while the back pair pushes down. Rustling sounds are caused by the wings touching together as the insect turns in the air.

Dragonflies are especially famous for their fast flight and dazzling feats in the air. They can twist and turn, change direction in an instant, hover in one place, dart up and down, and even fly backward! They can soar to great heights and travel long distances.

Damselflies are usually slower than dragonflies. They flutter along at a more leisurely pace while dragonflies often zip. But damselflies too can be fast and agile when the need arises.

Dragonflies and damselflies divide their lives between the two very different worlds of air and

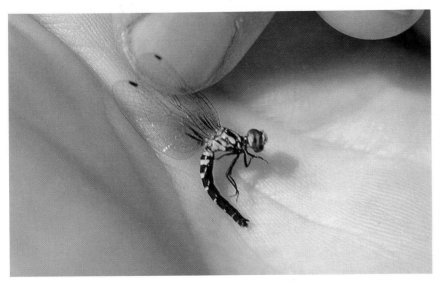

Top: Like all dragonflies, this clubtail is harmless to people. It's called a "dragon-hunter" because it often eats other dragonflies. Bottom left: The tiny elfin skimmer, or bluebell, is the smallest dragonfly found in North America. It looks like a wasp, which probably discourages birds from eating it. Bottom right: One of the longest damselflies is this five-inch one from Central America. It hovers in the air like a helicopter and plucks spiders from their webs.

water. As adults they sparkle in the sun and soar through the air. But their time of flying and brilliant colors is very short. It lasts only a few weeks or months. Most of a dragonfly's life is spent underwater as a dull-colored, wingless creature, hiding in the mud or among the weeds.

Although they look ferocious, dragonflies don't bite people and their long bodies have no stingers. They are dangerous only to mosquitoes and other tasty insects. In fact, they've been called "mosquito hawks" because they eat so many of these annoying pests.

Top: *Each of the dragonfly's huge eyes is made of over 20,000 tiny lenses. Dragonflies and damselflies rely on their keen eyesight to find mates and food and to return to the same perching spots time after time.* **Bottom:** *Some dragonflies catch and eat prey as large as themselves—even other dragonflies. This clubtail dragonfly is eating an immature one of the same kind.*

Dragonflies are fierce *predators* with bodies specialized for hunting and catching other flying insects. Huge eyes help them spot food from far away. Powerful wings and streamlined bodies let them whiz through the air to chase their prey. And they use their sharp, spiny legs and strong jaws to grab and devour their meals.

Mostly dragonflies eat small insects such as midges, gnats, mosquitoes and flies. But large dragonflies also catch bees, butterflies, moths and other dragonflies. Some huge Central American "helicopter" damselflies even snatch spiders right out of their webs.

A powdered dancer damselfly devours a small insect. The damselfly's flexible biting mouthparts can take in large hunks of food and tear them apart.

D ragonflies find their prey by sight. They can spot something moving as far as forty feet away. With huge eyes covering much of their heads and slender necks that can swivel in many directions, dragonflies have a very wide view of their surroundings.

Fast-moving dragonflies can speed along at thirty miles per hour on their large, lacy-looking wings. They may zoom even faster for short distances. Like stunt pilots they can dodge and dart and dive in all directions to catch even the swiftest and most agile prey. And when they collide with another insect during a high-speed chase, their bodies cushion the shock so they can keep on going without losing their balance.

Dragonflies can catch their prey in the air, using their thin, barbed legs. When food is sighted, the legs spread out to form a basket. With this the speeding dragonfly scoops up insects and transfers them to its mouth. Sometimes dragonflies just open their mouths as they fly, munching their way through a swarm of small insects. Their mouths may get so full of mosquitoes that they can't close their jaws.

While dragonflies often dine on the wing, damselflies usually land before eating. After a meal both dragonflies and damselflies may alight on a bush or a rock and carefully clean their faces with the tiny brushes on their front legs.

__Opposite__ (Page 8): Dewdrops sparkle on the colorful (and greatly magnified) back of a green darner dragonfly. __Bottom:__ Face to face with a green darner and its arsenal of hunting tools: enormous eyes, hooked jaws, and spiny legs. The legs are used for grabbing and holding rather than for walking.

Frogs, birds, and spiders are among the predators that eat dragonflies. **Bottom:** A hungry green frog lurks near a spot where dragonflies come to lay eggs. **Right:** A spider in its web captures an Eastern pondhawk dragonfly. **Opposite** (Page 11) **Top:** If they are too cold to fly, dragonflies and damselflies may warm up by basking in the sun or by vibrating their wings. Unable to move while covered with frost, this damselfly was warmed at last by the sun and flew away. **Center:** By pointing its rear end at the sun, this forceptail

dragonfly shades the rest of its body and keeps from getting too hot. **Bottom:** Guarding its streamside territory, this male rubyspot damselfly rises up on stilt legs to keep away from the hot rock.

10

D ragonflies themselves are sometimes eaten by frogs, spiders, and larger dragonflies. This is most likely to happen when the dragonflies are just emerging from the water, or when they're laying their eggs. At these times they're easy for predators to capture. Otherwise, adult dragonflies are not so easy to catch. Their wraparound vision usually alerts them to danger and they can fly quickly away.

Bad weather and extreme temperatures are also hazardous to dragonflies. Like snakes and frogs, insects are *cold-blooded.* That means that their body temperature depends on the temperature of the surroundings. If the weather is very chilly, dragonflies may be too cold to move. But they also need to avoid getting too hot. Some of their actions help them survive temperatures that aren't just right.

For example, if it's too cold to fly off and escape, a dragonfly may try to scare its enemy by raising its abdomen and flicking its wings. To warm up, a dragonfly flutters its wings or perches on a warm, sunny rock. If it's too hot, it can lower its wings to shade its body or point its abdomen at the sun so that it's less directly exposed to the heat.

When it rains or if it's windy, dragonflies often hide in sheltered places. And at night they often rest in groups, perched among the bushes and trees.

Top: *Courting candleflame skimmers. The male (left) holds up his abdomen to show off its bright colors and attract the female on the right.* **Bottom:** *Central American helicopter damselflies in tandem. The male is in front, holding on behind the female's head. Mating pairs may sometimes stay joined for several hours. They even fly while hooked together like this.*

Although they spend time feeding and resting in fields and treetops, dragonflies and damselflies must lay their eggs in or near the water. During their mating season they often return day after day to the same part of the pond or stream. There you may see them hovering around future mates, furiously chasing rivals, or hooked together in pairs with their bodies curved into bright-colored circles.

Many dragonflies stake out special territories for mating. Perched on a bush or patrolling the water's edge, the male guards his territory, keeping other males away and trying to mate with every female that comes along.

If another male shows up, the "owner" of the territory will charge fiercely, holding up his abdomen or wings to show their bright markings. The two males may take turns chasing back and forth until one of them gives up and leaves. Or they may fight by bashing into each other and whirling down in a noisy spiral.

When a female arrives the male may court her by showing off colored patches on his abdomen or wings. He may float on the water, or lead her down to an egg-laying spot. Then he flies down and grabs her by the head, holding on with special claspers at the end of his abdomen.

Orange bluet damselflies in tandem.

*During mating, the female loops her abdomen forward to receive sperm from the male. **Top:** Flame-tipped clubtail dragonflies. **Bottom:** Canyon rubyspot damselflies.*

One behind the other, the male and female fly around together. Some dragonflies actually mate while they're in the air. Others first land on a plant or a rock. There the female bends her abdomen forward so that the two dragonflies are linked in a loop. From a special pouch at the front of the male's abdomen, she receives some of his reproductive cells, or *sperm*. Stored in her body, these cells will fertilize the eggs she lays soon after mating. Each kind of dragonfly or damselfly has its own particular way of laying eggs. One uses the sharp end of her abdomen to

put eggs into a plant stem. Another simply lets eggs fall as she skims the pond surface, while a third pokes them into moist, soggy ground.

Some males stay with the female as she lays her eggs, guarding her by chasing other males away. Some even keep linked in their tandem position while the female goes underwater to deposit her eggs.

Most dragonflies and damselflies don't live long after mating and egg laying are done. But as their flying season is ending, the underwater life of a new generation is about to begin.

Still linked after mating, green darner dragonflies lay their eggs. With the sharp end of her abdomen, the female makes tiny holes in a plant stem and deposits an egg in each one. By keeping his hold on the female, the male prevents other males from trying to mate with her and interrupting the egg laying.

When the egg hatches, out comes a creature so ferocious and hungry that it is sometimes called a "pond monster." This *larva* or *nymph* is quite different from its colorful flying parents. It's dull brown or green, and has no wings. Its legs and antennae are longer, its head less moveable, and its eyes smaller than those of the adult. Although the full-grown dragonfly breathes air, the nymph has gills for taking oxygen from the water.

Before it can become an airborne adult, the nymph must survive in the pond or stream for months or even years, depending on which species it is. It lurks on the bottom or in the weeds, hiding from predators and snaring food like an underwater dragon.

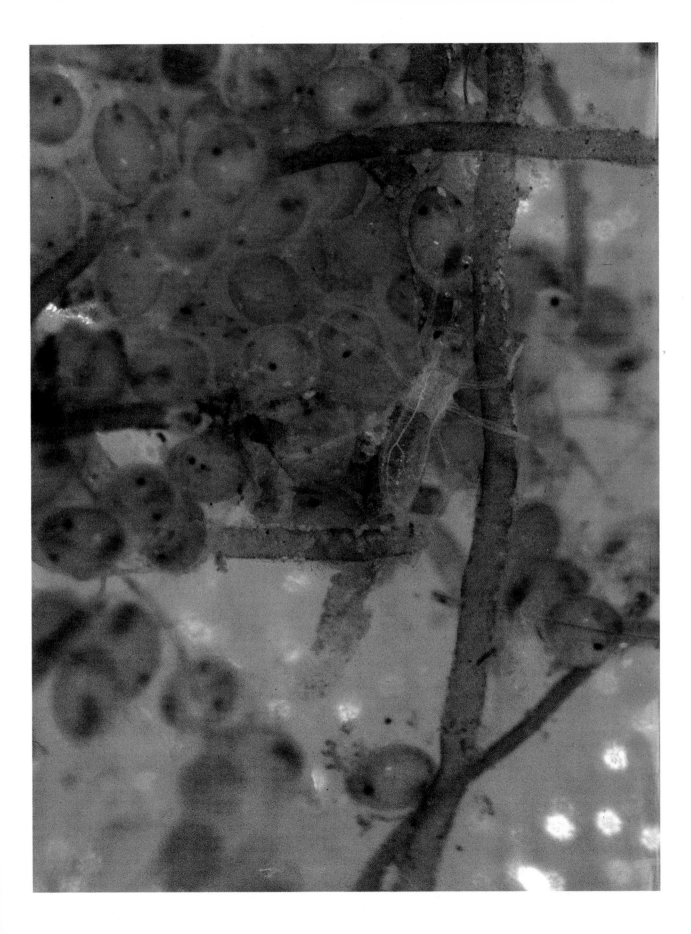

Top: *Dragonfly nymphs catch all kinds of small water animals. This one has a damselfly nymph sticking out of its ferocious jaws.* **Bottom:** *Greatly enlarged view of the lower lip or labium of an orange shadowfly nymph like the one above. The lip shoots out to grab food and pull it back to the nymph's mouth.*

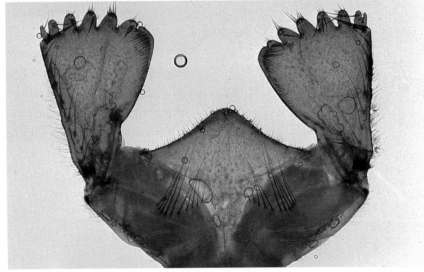

*L*ike its parents, the nymph is a hunter. But instead of swift and agile pursuit, it uses slow stalking and ambush to catch its prey.

Under the mud and debris the nymph lies motionless, waiting for a meal to come along. When a small animal moves into range, the nymph turns to face it. Suddenly the nymph's whole lower lip shoots away from its body. In less than a tenth of a second, sharp pincers on the lip grab the prey and pull it back to the nymph's mouth.

This remarkable lip, or *labium,* is one of the tools that make the "pond monster" such a fearsome hunter. Made of two hinged pieces attached to the head, it covers so much of the nymph's face that it is called a mask. Most of the time the labium is folded up under the head, but it shoots out to be half as long as the nymph's entire body.

Though clearly visible here on the sand, the dragonhunter nymph usually stays hidden among drifted leaves, where its flat shape and brown color make it hard to see.

Top: *With lightning speed, a darner nymph shoots out its deadly lower lip to catch a dobsonfly larva.* **Center:** *The gills of dragonfly nymphs are hidden inside their rear ends. With its very long abdomen sticking up into clear water, this clubtail nymph can breathe even when it burrows deep into the mud.* **Bottom:** *Damselfly nymphs have gills outside their bodies. The leaflike gills of this bluet nymph are easy to see on the end of its abdomen.*

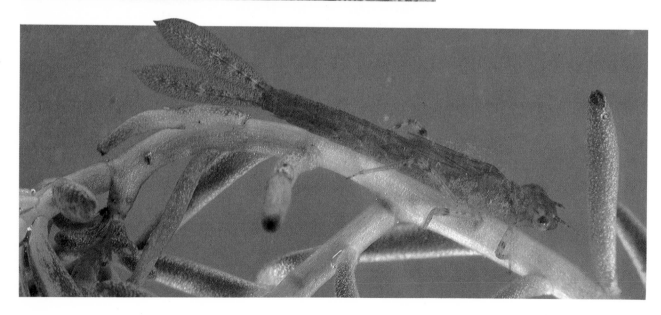

Dragonfly nymphs are greedy eaters. They will gobble up almost any living thing smaller than they are, and some will even attack creatures bigger than themselves. Mostly they live on small water insects and larvae, but as they get bigger, they can capture tadpoles, small fish, and even other nymphs.

The nymphs may be eaten by other animals, too. Their main protection is to stay hidden. But a threatened nymph may also dig rapidly into the bottom or cling more tightly to its weedy support. It may try to escape, or shoot out its lip and raise its abdomen in a frightening pose, or just play dead.

Nymphs tend to stay in one place or walk very slowly, but they can travel fast if they need to. The damselfly nymph can swim by moving its abdomen from side to side like a fish. The dragonfly nymph can squeeze water out of its rear end and shoot away like a jet, as fast as twenty inches per second.

In their underwater home, these small dragons are hard to see. But they're not too hard to catch and observe. Along the edge of a pond or stream, search among the weeds and scoop up sand or mud with an old kitchen strainer. Or put the strainer or a net across a narrow place in the stream and rile up the bottom by picking up rocks or stirring around with a stick. Then dump the contents of the scoop into a flat white pan of water. Along with gravel and mud, small water animals and bits of plants, you may find a "pond monster" dragonfly or damselfly nymph.

The nymph of the shining clubtail dragonfly spends most of its time burrowed into clean sand at the bottom of a stream.

The twin-spotted spiketail nymph hunts by lying in wait, hidden in the sand. Only its head shows as it devours a captured damselfly nymph.

After watching the nymph for a while you'll probably want to put it back in the water. But you may be able to raise it in an aquarium, if you provide plenty of food and an environment as much as possible like its home. You can feed the nymph small insects or larvae, or mealworms from a pet store. Be sure to provide a stick or stem so the nymph can crawl out of the water when it is ready to change into an adult.

Most nymphs take about two years to grow into adults. During this time the nymph outgrows its skin and sheds it, or *molts*, ten or fifteen times. Each time it molts the nymph comes out a little bit changed. It gets bigger, wing pads appear, and the eyes develop.

As the time for the big change, or *metamorphosis*, comes closer, the nymph's behavior changes, too. It needs more oxygen, so its breathing speeds up, and it may leave the water to get air. Nymphs that live in deep water move closer to shore.

A few days before it's time to emerge, the nymph stops eating. Its jaw dissolves and begins to change into the jaw of an adult. Finally, the nymph selects a stick or a stem, climbs out of the water, and clings there, waiting.

Top right: *Nymphs outgrow and shed their hard outer coverings several times before becoming adults. The jade clubtail nymph has just come out of its old skin on the left.* **Bottom:** *Nymph of a twelve-spotted skimmer eating a worm.*

Lots of dangers await emerging dragonflies. Birds search the pond's edge, picking up one after another of the helpless, newly-hatched adults. Or, there may be so many nymphs emerging at one time that some get jostled off the stems they've climbed and are unable to get back out of the water. Cold weather may slow down or stop their final molting, or wind may damage their weak new wings. But some will survive to leave their watery life, flying off into the sunlight until it's time to lay their own eggs.

The cycle of a dragonfly's life has been repeated over and over again for millions of years. Although their environment has changed, dragonflies and damselflies have continued to find food and to escape danger, to mate and to lay eggs. They have been able to adapt and survive.

As hunters that eat many kinds of insects, dragonflies are not likely to run out of food. Even if one kind of insect dies out or disappears, they can always find plenty of others to eat.

The adults need warmth to be able to move and reproduce, but their eggs and larvae can survive the cold. The eggs can even survive dryness and drought until there's enough water for them to hatch. The nymphs have gills for breathing, but if there's not enough oxygen in the water they can climb up a stem and breathe in the air.

In the different environments where they live, each kind of dragonfly or damselfly has developed special ways of surviving. Some dragonflies lay eggs in waterfalls or fast-flowing water, and their nymphs are adapted for holding on tight so they won't be swept away by the current. Nymphs that live in still or slow-moving water have flat, hairy shapes that keep them from sinking too deep in the mud where they lie buried.

Opposite (Page 24) **Top:** *Climbing among the water plants, the nymph of the comet darner dragonfly stalks its prey like a cat. This one is in the very last stage before becoming an adult.* **Bottom:** *Out of the water and into the air, this recently emerged jade club-tail dragonfly will soon leave its old skin behind and fly off to begin its brief adult life.*

A widow skimmer. Dragonflies much like this one have been soaring through the air since the time of the dinosaurs.

25

But dragonflies haven't adapted to some of the human-caused changes in their environment. They have become scarce and have even disappeared from some areas where the water has been polluted or where marshes and swamps have been filled in for new building. Like all animals, dragonflies can survive only if they have a suitable place to live.

Every season for millions of years, enough adults have survived to lay enough eggs to hatch into enough nymphs to grow into enough adults to keep the process going again and again. And wherever there are ponds and streams of clean water, dragonflies and damselflies still soar through the air on their spectacular wings, sparkling in the sunshine.

As its ancestors have done for millions of years, a damselfly waits at dawn for the warmth and light of the rising sun.

PHOTO ACKNOWLEDGMENTS

A note about names:

Many dragonflies do not have familiar common names. Most of the names in the photo captions were taken from a list compiled by Dennis R. Paulson and Sidney W. Dunkle. Scientific names when known by the photographers are listed below.

Page iii: Roseate Skimmer, *orthemis ferruginea*, Curtis E. Williams.

Page iv: *Neurocordulia xanthosoma*, Curtis E. Williams.

Page 2: Top: *Belonia croceipennis*, Curtis E. Williams. Center: *Gomphoides albrighti*, Curtis E. Williams. Bottom: *Libellula pulchella*, Bill Ivy.

Page 3: Top: *Calopteryx dimidiata*, Curtis E. Williams. Center: *Argia extranea*, Dennis Paulson. Bottom: *Telebasis salva*, Curtis E. Williams.

Page 4: *Perithemis tenera*, Curtis E. Williams.

Page 5: Top: *Hagenius brevistylus*, Sid Dunkle. Bottom left: *Nannothemis bella*, Sid Dunkle. Bottom right: *Mecistogaster linearis*, Ola M. Fincke.

Page 6: Top: *Pachydiplax longipennis*, Curtis E. Williams. Bottom: *Gomphus sp.*, Ola M. Fincke.

Page 7: *Argia moesta*, Curtis E. Williams.

Page 8: *Anax junius*, Frank Cocco.

Page 9: *Anax junius*, Bill Ivy.

Page 10: Left: Ola M. Fincke. Right: *Erythemis simplicicollis*, Curtis E. Williams.

Page 11: Top: Bill Ivy. Center: *Aphylla williamsoni*, Michael May. Bottom: *Hetaerina vulnerata*, John Alcock.

Page 12: Top: *Belonia croceipennis*, Curtis E. Williams. Bottom: *Megaloprepus coerulatus*, Ola M. Fincke.

Page 13: *Enallagma signatum*, Michael May.

Page 14: Top: *Gomphus militaris*, Curtis E. Williams. Bottom: *Hetaerina vulnerata*, John Alcock.

Page 15: *Anax junius*, Curtis E. Williams.

Page 16: *Gomphus submedianus*, Curtis E. Williams.

Page 17: *Belonia croceipennis*, Curtis E. Williams.

Page 18: Top and bottom: *Neurocordulia xanthosoma*, Curtis E. Williams.

Page 19: *Hagenius brevistylus*, Sid Dunkle.

Page 20: Top: *Boyeria sp.*, Frank Cocco. Center: *Phyllocycla volsella*, Dennis Paulson. Bottom: *Enallagma sp.*, Curtis E. Williams.

Page 21: *Stylurus ivae*, Sid Dunkle.

Page 22: *Cordulegaster maculatus*, Curtis E. Williams.

Page 23: Top: *Gomphus submedianus*, Bottom: *Libellula pulchella*, Curtis E. Williams.

Page 24: Top: *Anax longipes*, Sid Dunkle. Bottom: *Gomphus submedianus*, Curtis E. Williams.

Page 25: *Libellula luctuosa*, Frank Cocco.

Page 27: Bill Ivy.